Note to Parents and Teachers

The READING ABOUT: STARTERS series introduces key science vocabulary to young children while encouraging them to discover and understand the world around them. The series works as a set of graded readers in three levels.

LEVEL 1: BEGINNING TO READ follows guidelines set out in the National Curriculum for Year 1 in schools. These books can be read alone or as part of guided or group reading. Each book has three sections:

• Information pages that introduce new words. These key words appear in bold throughout the book for easy recognition.
• A lively story that recalls this vocabulary and encourages children to use these words when they talk and write.
• A quiz and picture index ask children to look back and recall what they have read.

DIGGERS AND TOOLS AT WORK looks at MACHINES. Below are some answers related to the questions on the information spreads that parents, carers and teachers can use to discuss and develop further ideas and concepts:

p. 5 *What other jobs can machines do?* Encourage children to think about machines in groups, e.g. machines that clean (washing machine, roadsweeper), carry us (cars, buses and trains), help us keep in touch (e.g. telephones), or entertain us (TVs, radios, toys).

p. 7 *What other fast machines can you think of?* You could group these by land, sea and air, e.g. cars, ambulances; speedboats and hovercraft; planes and helicopters.

p. 9 *Why should you be careful with sharp tools?* Remind children not to touch knives, saws, chisels and other sharp tools and to be very careful when handling scissors.

p. 11 *What other machines have wheels?* Point out that as well as machines that roll along, from tractors and cars to shopping trolleys and skateboards, objects such as roundabouts, doorknobs and ferris wheels also spin like a wheel.

p. 13 *What does an engine need to give it energy?* Engines need fuel to give them energy. The motor in an electric machine needs electricity from a socket or a battery.

p. 17 *Why does a train need a very strong engine?* Reinforce the idea that big machines need more power, e.g. a jumbo jet has much more powerful engines than a small plane.

p. 19 *How do you dig a hole? Are you as fast as a digger?* You can dig a big hole with a bucket and spade, but a powerful engine helps a machine dig much faster.

p. 21 *What boats move on water without an engine?* Sailing boats and windsurfers are pushed along by the wind. You move rowing boats or canoes using oars and paddles.

ADVISORY TEAM

Educational Consultant
Andrea Bright – Science Co-ordinator, Trafalgar Junior School, Twickenham

Literacy Consultant
Jackie Holderness – former Principal Lecturer in Primary Education, Westminster Institute, Oxford Brookes University

Series Consultants
Anne Fussell – Early Years Teacher and University Tutor, Westminster Institute, Oxford Brookes University

David Fussell – C.Chem., FRSC

CONTENTS

© Aladdin Books Ltd 2006

Designed and produced by
Aladdin Books Ltd
2/3 Fitzroy Mews
London W1T 6DF

First published in
Great Britain in 2006 by
Franklin Watts
96 Leonard Street
London EC2A 4XD

A catalogue record for this book is available from the British Library.

ISBN 0 7496 6254 9

Printed in Malaysia

All rights reserved

Editor: Sally Hewitt

Design: Flick, Book Design and Graphics

Picture research:
Alexa Brown

Thanks to:
• The pupils of Trafalgar Infants School, Twickenham for appearing as models in this book.
• Debbie Staynes for helping to organise the photoshoots.
• The pupils and teachers of Trafalgar Junior School, Twickenham and St. Nicholas C.E. Infant School, Wallingford, for testing the sample books.

Photocredits:
l-left, r-right, b-bottom, t-top, c-centre, m-middle
Front cover tl, 8t, 32mlt — USDA. Front cover tm, 7 both, 20t, 32mrb — Scania. Front cover tr, 2tl, 9, 10, 12b, 31ml, 32mrt — US Navy. Front cover b, 3, 5t, 11t, 13, 18, 22tr, 31br, 32ml, 32br — John Deere. 2ml, 4b, 11br, 31tr, 32tl — Renault. 2bl, 20br, 23tr, 32mlb & bl — Digital Vision. 4tr, 6b, 16br, 17, 19, 22b, 26ml, 28ml, 29t, 31mr, 32tr — Corbis. 6b, 12tr — TongRo. 6tr, 15ml — Ingram Publishing. 8br, 15tr, 24-25 all, 28bl, 30tl — Marc Arundale / Select Publishing. 14bl, 15br, 26tr, 30mr, 32mr — Jim Pipe. 14br — Comstock. 16t — Digital Vision. 21 — NASA. 23b, 29b — PBD. 27t — Select Pictures. 27br — Photodisc. 28tl — Corel.

MACHINES

Diggers and Tools at Work

by Jim Pipe

Aladdin/Watts
London • Sydney

Everywhere you go, **machines** are at **work**.

Cars and trucks help us to move about.

Tractors **work** on a farm.

Diggers **work** on the roads.

Some **machines** are just for fun!

• What other jobs can machines do?

How do machines help us?

Tools help us to
do small jobs.

A big truck is very **strong**.
It can do heavy jobs.

6

A bus
goes **fast**.
It can take
us a long
way.

A fire engine comes **fast** to keep us safe.

• What other fast machines can you think of?

Scissors

Tools help us
to make things.

We **hit** a nail with a hammer.
We **cut** paper with scissors.

We push and pull a saw to **cut** wood.

Many **tools** are sharp.
They are made from metal.

• Why should you be careful with sharp tools?

Bicycle

Many machines have **wheels.**

Wheels make it easy to move.
They **roll** along the ground.

10

Track

Wheels and tracks can **roll** over bumpy ground.

A driver **turns** a **wheel** to go left or right.

• What other machines have wheels?

Some machines have no **engine**.

We push the pedals to make a bicycle move.

We push a wheelbarrow.

Many machines have an **engine**.

The **engine** pushes and pulls.
It makes the wheels go round.

Engine

• *What does an engine need to give it energy?*

Electric machines do jobs at home.
Motors make them push and pull.

Electric machines clean floors.
They also wash clothes and dishes.

Vacuum cleaner

Dishwasher

A **motor** helps
a CD player
play music.

A **motor** makes
the hands on
an **electric**
clock move.

A **motor** makes an
electric toy move.

• What other machines and tools do jobs at home?

Machines with engines and wheels **carry** us about.
A car can **carry** a whole family.

A bus can **carry** a whole class.

A train pulls lots of coaches.
It can **carry** a whole school!

A train has lots of wheels.
Its strong engine has a lot of **power**.

• Why does a train need a very strong engine?

Some machines are made for hard work.

A digger uses tools to **dig** and carry.
Wheels and tracks help it move.
Its strong engine has lots of power.

Digger

Diggers, trucks and cranes
help us **build** roads and houses.

What is this crane trying to **lift**?

Crane

• *How do you dig a hole? Are you as fast as a digger?*

Machines can move
on land, sea and air.

A boat **floats**
on water.

A plane can **fly**
in the air.

A rocket can **fly** into space!

• What boats move on water without an engine?

Big machines
need a **driver**.

A **driver controls**
a digger.

A pilot **controls** a plane.

You can **control** machines, too.

You pull a rope to steer a go-kart.

You push a button to switch on an electric machine.

Television

• What machine would you like to drive?

NOISY MACHINE!

Read the story and look out
for words about **machines**.

Dad is using his
electric power tool.

It **works fast,**
but it is very noisy!

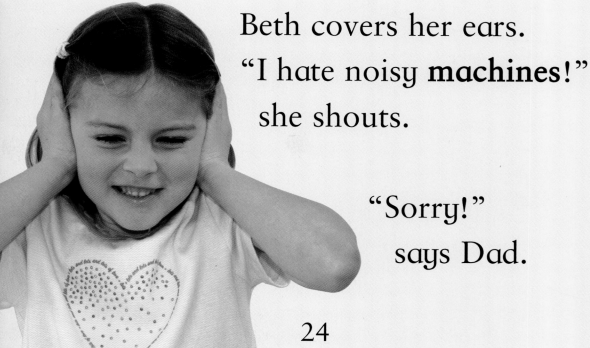

Beth covers her ears.
"I hate noisy **machines!**"
she shouts.

"Sorry!"
says Dad.

Dan doesn't mind.

He likes **electric** toys with noisy **motors.**

He loves to watch big diggers at **work.**

"Let's go to the park. It will be quiet there," says Dad.

"The washing **machine** can clean my smelly socks while we are out!"

On the way, a big
bus drives past.

"Smelly **machine!**"
says Beth.

Dan waves
at the **driver**.
He likes **machines**
with **wheels**.

He'd love to ride
a **fast** motorbike!

"Look over there, Dan," says Dad.
"What are those **machines building?**"

Diggers are **digging** a big hole.

A crane is **lifting** a heavy load.

"Noisy **machines!**" says Beth. "Let's go!"

At the park, skaters **roll** along the path.

"Are skates **machines?**" asks Dan.

"Yes," says Beth.

"They have **wheels.**"

A sailing boat is **floating** on the lake.

It has no **engine**. "At last, a quiet **machine!**" says Beth.

Dan sees some kites. "They **fly** without an **engine**," he says.

"You **control** a kite by pulling on the string," says Dad.

A big plane **flies** by.
"Noisy **machine!**" shouts Beth.

They walk to the playground.
"You'll like these **machines**, Beth!"
laughs Dad.

They play on the
roundabout. It
spins like a **wheel**.

Dan and Beth **carry** home food for dinner. Dad **cuts** up the food with a knife.

Beth switches on her CD player. Dad covers his ears. "Noisy **machine!**" he laughs.

Look around your home or school. What jobs are **machines** doing?

Draw a picture of a **machine**. Write a label to say what it is.

Car

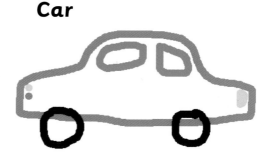

QUIZ

What **machines work** on a farm?

Answer on page 4

What are sharp **tools** made of?

Answer on page 9

Can a train **carry** more than a car?

Answer on page 17

Who **controls** a digger?

Answer on page 22

Did you know the answers? Give yourself a

Do you remember these words about **machines**?
Well done! Can you remember any more?

work

page 4

strong

page 6

tool

page 8

wheel

page 10

engine

page 13

motor

page 15

carry

page 16

float

page 20

fly

page 20

driver

page 22